Horrible Harry Goes to Sea

BY SUZY KLINE

Pictures by Frank Remkiewicz

SCHOLASTIC INC.

New York   Toronto   London   Auckland   Sydney
Mexico City   New Delhi   Hong Kong   Buenos Aires

As always, special thanks to my editor, Cathy Hennessy, for helping me create this book, to the third graders at Southwest School in Torrington, Connecticut, who went with me on the riverboat at Essex in the spring of 2000, and to Snyder-Goosen's Second Grade Sailors in Fairport, New York. I love my honorary sailor's hat. It was great to be on board at Dudley Elementary for a week. Keep sailing through school!

ISBN 0-439-52000-2

Text copyright © 2001 by Suzy Kline.
Illustrations copyright © 2001 by Frank Remkiewicz. All rights reserved.
Published by Scholastic Inc., 557 Broadway, New York, NY 10012, by arrangement with Viking Children's Books, a member of Penguin Putnam Inc. SCHOLASTIC and associated logos are trademarks and/or registered trademarks of Scholastic Inc.

12 11 10 9 8 7 6 5 4 3 2   3 4 5 6 7 8/0

Printed in the U.S.A.   40

First Scholastic printing, January 2003

Set in New Century Schoolbook

Dedicated to my first granddaughter,
Mikenna Rose Hurtuk,
who just came ashore February 18, 2001,
in Rockville, Connecticut.

I love you, Grandma Sue

Contents

Ancestors

My name is Doug. I'm in third grade. I write stories about things that happen in Room 3B. Usually, the stories are about Harry, who likes to do horrible things, or Song Lee, the nicest person in our class.

I never thought I'd write about Ida.

I mean, why would I?

She hardly says anything.

She plays with Song Lee and Mary.

She takes dance lessons after school.

She wears her hair in a ponytail that looks like a neat bush on top of her head.

Big deal.

Well, one morning in November, we found out something about Ida that none of us knew before. I couldn't believe it! No one could.

It all started on a Tuesday, when Ida walked into class carrying a black box. It was about the size of a loaf of bread.

"Ooooh," Mary oohed. "A box with a lock. What's inside?"

"You'll see," Ida replied as she walked over to her desk. The bush on her head bounced around like it was in a wind storm.

Mary followed her. "Does that little key you're wearing open the lock on your black box?"

"Yes," Ida said, fooling with her gold necklace. "*This* key opens it up."

Now four of us stared at the gold key.

"*Open it!*" Sidney shouted.

"Yeah," Harry agreed. "Maybe there's a snake inside."

"Ida." Mary quivered. "Is there something . . . *horrible* in that box?"

Before Ida could reply, the bell rang.

"Please be seated," Miss Mackle said.

After the Pledge of Allegiance, and lunch count, the teacher announced, "Boys and girls, it's time to share our homework."

I opened my backpack. Just about everybody put something on their desk. Even Harry, but it was too small to see what it was.

"Boys and girls," the teacher said, "For the past few days we have been talking about our *ancestors*. Who can explain what that word means?"

"It means our dead relatives," Harry blurted out. Then he flashed his white teeth.

While Miss Mackle made a face, Mary reworded things. "Ancestors are people in our family who lived before us. They are our family roots . . . our family tree."

"Thank you, Mary," the teacher replied. "You know class, when we learn about our ancestors, we learn more about ourselves. For homework, you were to talk to your parents about your ancestors, and bring something to class about one of them. Who would like to go first?"

Everyone's hand went up except Song Lee's and Ida's. I expected Song Lee not to raise her hand. She was shy about going up in front of the class. But I had no idea why Ida didn't raise hers. So I asked.

"I want to be last," she whispered back. "Mine is really special." I nodded as she squeezed her gold key.

"Me! Me! Me!" Sidney called out,

waving his hand in the air as if he had just fallen in the middle of a frozen lake.

"Sidney," Miss Mackle replied calmly.

Sid raced up to the front of the room and put a patch over his left eye. "My grandmother told me about our family tree. And three hundred years ago one of my ancestors was a pirate! His name was Rupert, and he had red hair just like me. He sailed off the coast of Cape Cod. Isn't that cool?"

Everyone raised their eyebrows. Even Harry. It was definitely cool.

Sidney continued. "My grandmother also told me the reason why he wore one gold earring. When a pirate dies and is washed ashore, whoever finds his dead body is supposed to dig him a

grave and bury him. The gold earring pays for the guy's hard work."

"Fascinating!" Miss Mackle exclaimed.

"Was Rupert's dead body washed ashore?" Harry asked.

"No," Sidney groaned. "Grandma said when his ship docked one day, he met a woman named Rose, married her, and wasn't a pirate anymore. Bummer."

"Bummer," Harry agreed.

When it was Mary's turn, she unfolded a quilt. "My great-grandmother Gilda made this in Israel. Her family saved scraps of cloth and sewed them together to make blankets. Mom said they didn't waste anything."

"It's so colorful!" Miss Mackle exclaimed.

I went up next. "My great-grandfather

Benjamin was president of a bank in Indiana. He was real good with numbers. But Mom told me there was something called the Great Depression in 1930 and his bank closed. He was sad about that."

Then I showed everyone my piggy

bank. "Grandfather Ben gave this to my mom and she gave it to me. I save my pennies and nickels in it now."

After I sat down, it was Harry's turn.

He held up a dog tag on a long silver chain. "This belonged to my great-grandfather Sam Spooger. He was a captain in World War II. Mom said when he was in Italy, an artillery shell fell off the rack. Right in front of ten army men!

"Those huge bullets are heavier than a bowling ball! If one of those babies hit the ground, you'd be blasted to smithereens. Well, my great-grandfather caught it with his bare hands before it touched the ground. He saved his men, but he lost his thumb. He was a hero."

Miss Mackle put her hand over her heart and sighed.

When Song Lee went up to the front of the room, she spoke in a soft voice. Slowly, she opened her big bag. "My great-grandfather Chung Hee Park was a painter. He painted this picture of the countryside in South Korea where my family lived. *Korea* means land of high mountains and sparkling streams. And that is what Great-Grandfather Chung Hee liked to paint."

Song Lee finally smiled as she headed for her seat. I think she was relieved her turn was over.

"Thank you for sharing your ancestor's beautiful painting!" Miss Mackle said. "And thank you, boys and girls, for sharing such inspiring stories!"

Finally, Miss Mackle called the last person. "Ida?"

Ida picked up the black box and walked to the front of the room.

Everyone sat up and waited to find out what was inside her locked box.

Ida's Box

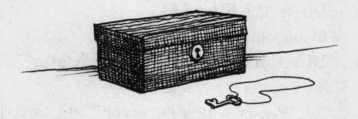

We all watched Ida use the key on her gold necklace to unlock the box. When it clicked, our eyes doubled in size.

But instead of opening the box, she pulled down our world map. "My great-great-grandmother," Ida said, "was born here in India." Everyone looked at the country she pointed to. "It kind of looks like an ice cream cone."

Everyone leaned forward as Ida slowly removed the lid from her black box. "Her name was Persis, and she sailed on the *Titanic*!"

"Ooooooh," everyone oohed.

"Did Purse die in the icy water?" Sidney asked.

"No, *Persis* was a survivor," Ida said proudly. "The things in this black box

are replicas. Mom told me that means copies. They're not the originals. But it gives you an idea of what it was like to be on the *Titanic*. There are postcards, and a menu, and even telegrams warning about the icebergs."

"Ooooooh," we oohed again.

Miss Mackle closed her grade book.

"Amazing! Your great-great-grandmother sailed on the *Titanic*!"

"She was a dancer like me," Ida added with a big grin. "She danced in the *general room* until midnight. That's where the third-class passengers played instruments."

"Rupert sang sea chanteys like *yo ho ho and a bottle of rum*!" Sidney blurted out.

"If Elvis was there, he'd be playing his guitar," Dexter chimed in. Then he shuffled his feet and tapped his fingers on his desk.

Mary snapped at both Sidney and Dexter, "Shhhh! It's *not* your turn!"

Ida continued, "Great-Great-Grandmother Persis was 98 years old when she died. I don't remember her because

I was just a baby then. But Mom showed me her scrapbook. When she finally got to America, she met my great-great-grandfather in New York City. He was an African-American. My ancestors are from India and Africa."

Harry left his seat without permission and got the *T* encyclopedia. I knew he was looking up the *Titanic*.

"When she was on the lifeboat, she sang a lot," Ida added. "Mom told me it helped calm the people."

Five minutes later, when we were still talking about the *Titanic*, Harry found what he was looking for. *"Here it is!"*

Everyone shot out of their seat and ran over to Harry. Miss Mackle didn't say anything. She came over too.

"Look at that big baby!" Harry exclaimed. "It covers two pages. It says the *Titanic* was as long as four city blocks. Hey, Doug, that's how far it is from my house to your house."

"Wow," I sighed.

While some of us gathered around Harry, others gathered around Ida to look at the postcards, menus, and telegrams.

"Who would like to go to the library and check out some books on the *Titanic*?" Miss Mackle asked.

Six of us darted over to her desk for the green library passes. Little did we know that Ida's box would take us to sea, *ourselves*!

All Aboard!

That morning six of us rushed to the library and checked out books on the *Titanic*. When there were no more, our librarian, Mrs. Michaelsen, suggested Harry and I look at a book on the *Mayflower*. "That's a great ship too," she said. Then she helped Sidney find one about a pirate ship.

"Thanks!" we replied, and we took

the books back to class.

The rest of that morning we drew pictures of ships and collected facts about them. Song Lee and Mary and Ida used Magic Markers to make a giant *Titanic* ship. They used a map from Ida's box to draw the rooms. They even made the Turkish bath room and the smoking room. Song Lee used a ruler.

Sidney kept singing *yo ho ho and a bottle of rum*. Then he made up his own verses:

A pirate's tough but he can sing.
He wears a patch and a gold earring.
He climbs up rope and sails the sea
With a yo ho ho and a yo ho hee!

Harry and I clapped. "Not bad, Sid the Squid," Harry said. Then we got back to work.

"Let's make a list of numbers about the *Mayflower*," I suggested.

"Neato," Harry said, taking a stub pencil from behind his ear.

"Here's two," I said. "The *Mayflower* set sail in 1620, and there were 102 passengers on board."

"Here's another: a storm lasted 14 days," Harry said.

"The Pilgrims were on the ship for 65 days," I added.

"Here's the poop deck," Harry said. "See? It's this top deck. That's probably where they went to the bathroom."

"Nope. Not there," I said. "I read about it. When they had to go to the bathroom, they did it downstairs in chamber pots."

Harry thought about it for a minute. Then he called out, "Hey, Ida! Did your great-great-grandmother have a chamber pot!"

Ida stopped coloring. "Yes, she did. It looked like a big porcelain vase with a lid, and had flowers on it. It was a beautiful potty."

As soon as Song Lee started giggling, Ida and Mary did too. Then they added a chamber pot to their drawing.

"Hey Sid!" Harry hollered. "Where did pirates go to the bathroom?"

Sidney pointed at something in his pirate's book. It looked like a see-saw, but half of it was hanging over the water.

"See this wooden plank with big holes in it?"

We nodded.

"That's it!" Sid replied. "Pirates sat on it. They went to the bathroom right into the ocean."

"Eeyeew!" most of us groaned.

Suddenly Harry jumped up. "You know what we should do?"

No one said anything.

"We should set sail on the sea!" Harry held his hands up high and then made a three-finger salute.

Mary stopped drawing the library room of the *Titanic*. "What? Room 3B go to sea?"

Harry shrugged. "Why not?" Then he raced over to the plastic tub of brochures Miss Mackle kept about our state. "I saw it in here somewhere."

"What?" Sidney asked.

"What?" Mary repeated.

They were both standing over Harry while he rummaged around. Finally he pulled out a bright red-and-blue brochure. There was a picture of a riverboat on the cover. *"This!"*

Miss Mackle came over. "Oh, yes, that's the riverboat at Essex. It cruises up and down the Connecticut River."

"Oooooooh," Ida replied, looking at the picture of the riverboat with the two red, white, and black smokestacks. "I wish we could go to sea, too!"

"Why not?" Harry said.

Mary brought up one reason. "Because it costs money. We would have to pay for the bus and boat."

"That's true," I agreed.

Miss Mackle picked up the brochure and looked at the schedule for late fall trips. "Actually, we have money left in our field trip fund. "We could . . . go to sea. Lots of our ancestors did."

Harry and Ida started jumping up and down.

The rest of Room 3B cheered.

"Let's do it!" Miss Mackle exclaimed.

"All aboard!" Ida and Harry called.

The Missing Earring

November 24 was the day we set sail. We met at 7:30 A.M. in front of the school. It was dark enough for Harry to use his pocket flashlight. When he saw me, he shined it in my face. "Sit with you on the bus," he said.

"Sure," I said. I was counting on it. Then I noticed what Harry was wearing. An orange life jacket.

"Where did you get that thing?" I asked.

Harry patted his life jacket and then secured the buckle. "I got it at a tag sale with my own money. Cool, huh?"

"Cool." Then we slapped each other five.

Ida's mother, Mrs. Burrell, was one of the six chaperones. Miss Mackle was happy she was coming along because Mrs. Burrell was a nurse. Ida and her mother both had yellow raincoats on.

Sidney's stepdad got on the bus with Sidney. Mr. La Fleur was wearing a pith helmet and a black jacket with silver letters on the back that said: George La Fleur TOMBSTONES.

Sidney had a pen and a pad

of paper. He was drawing a pirate ship.

Just before the bus took off, Miss Mackle passed out white sailor hats for everyone to wear. Each hat had our name printed on the front in black ink. "I couldn't resist these," she exclaimed. "I got them on special at the Army

Navy store. They'll make great name tags!"

"*Yahoo!*" we all yelled as we pulled them down over our heads.

During the bus ride, Harry and I chatted.

"Have you ever gone to sea before?" I asked.

"Nope."

"Me neither," I said.

Mary stuck her head over the back of our bus seat. "We're not really going to sea," she snapped. "We're going on the river. The Connecticut River."

"The Connecticut River empties into Long Island Sound and that goes right into the ocean," Harry snapped. "It's all the same thing. We're going to sea!"

Mary rolled her eyeballs, "Okay,

Captain Spooger, I'm going to sea for a second time."

Harry grinned. He liked being called Captain.

"What do you mean second time? You've gone to sea, Mary?"

"Once I took a ferry to the Statue of

Liberty. That's where a lot of our ancestors sailed to."

Miss Mackle beamed. I could tell she was glad the word "ancestors" had popped up in our conversation.

"There were lots of waves," Mary added. "The boat really rocked back and forth, like this." Everyone watched Mary jostle Song Lee and herself backward and forward.

"It was kind of . . . scary," she added in a soft voice.

Song Lee joined the conversation. I wondered why she was wearing just one gold hoop earring, but I didn't ask. "When I was four," she said, "I sailed on a ship from Korea to San Francisco."

"Whoa," Harry groaned. "That's going to sea *big time!*"

"What was it like crossing the Pacific Ocean?" I asked.

Song Lee smiled. "I felt safe sitting on Mother's lap. I smelled sea air and watched our ship make big waves. Once when we had dinner, my plate slid right off the table."

Sidney interrupted. "Hey, you guys, maybe we'll discover Captain Kidd's pirate treasure. They say it's buried somewhere along the shore of the Connecticut River." Suddenly, Sidney leaned over and tied his boots. When he sat back up, he was beaming like *he* had just found a treasure himself!

"You know Sid," Harry replied, "if you were a pirate captain, they'd call you Captain Squid!"

Just as Sidney held up a fist, Mary

screamed, *"Song Lee's gold earring is missing!"*

Miss Mackle immediately turned around. "I'll tell the bus driver," she replied. "If we don't find it, the bus company will."

"It's okay," Song Lee said.

When Harry and I noticed her eyes filling up with tears, we knew she was sad about it.

"Hey, Song Lee," Sidney called. "Now *you* can be a pirate going to sea with one earring!"

Mary made a face. "Thanks, Sid. That really cheers her up."

Room 3B Sets Sail!

When we arrived at Essex, we could see the big riverboat docked at the pier through our bus window. It was exciting to see the red, white, and black smokestacks.

"I'm sorry about your earring," Mary said to Song Lee. "I bet it fell off when we were rocking on the bus."

"I'll look for it while you're gone," the

bus driver said as we walked by. "You'd be surprised what I find on my bus."

"Thank you," Song Lee replied.

Ida changed the subject. "Look," she said. "There must be ten other classes here. Don't you feel like you're boarding the *Titanic*? We even have our own green passenger tickets."

Song Lee nodded as she pulled her sailor's hat further down over her head. Harry pointed to the top deck. "Let's make sure we get up there so we can see stuff. We want to go first class!"

"Single file please," Miss Mackle ordered.

Mr. La Fleur followed at the rear of the line with Sidney. He kept calling, "All aboard! All aboard!" Mrs. Burrell was in the middle. She had a first aid kit. As we stepped onto the gangplank, I started to get excited. "Just think, we're going on a ship just like the Pilgrims and those people on the *Titanic*."

"And like the pirates!" Sid added.

"Downstairs, please," one of the shipmen said. "The top deck is full."

"Rats!" Harry groaned. "That's no fair. I wanted to be on the top deck. That's where the action is!"

When we walked down the stairs, I made a face too. "Gee, it's like being in third class on the *Titanic*."

"Most people were," Ida replied, "including my great-great-grandmother. She went third class."

Mrs. Burrell smiled as she put a Band Aid on Mary's finger. Mary's ticket had just given her a papercut.

"Everyone take a seat please, we're ready to cast off!" the captain announced over the loudspeaker.

Harry and I scooted into a row of chairs next to a porthole. "Can you see the water?" I asked.

Harry pressed his nose against the glass. "Look, Doug! It's like a war movie. There are floating bombs all over the place."

"Bombs?" I pushed Harry aside and looked out the porthole. "Those aren't bombs, they're buoys."

"Well, they look like bombs," Harry said in a disappointed voice. "And they look like they're moving."

"We're the ones moving," I explained.

"All clear," the captain said over the loudspeaker. "You can leave your seats now."

Song Lee and Ida jumped up and started walking across the lower deck.

"Some voyage," Harry grumbled. "I can't even smell the sea air down here."

"Look," I said, peering out the window. "There's a big water bird's nest on top of that buoy."

Harry shined his flashlight on it. "Cool," he said. "Maybe we'll spot another one down the river."

"Want to get postcards?" Ida asked Mary and Song Lee. "They sell them on the ship. I want to add them to my collection."

"Yes!" the girls replied. Mrs. Burrell followed the girls to the souvenir and snack shop.

Harry made a face. "Postcards, shmostcards. I want to go on the top deck."

"I'll take you up there," Mr. La Fleur said.

"I'm hungry," Sidney complained.

"Can I get something at the snack shop first?"

"Tell you what," Mr. La Fleur said. "Mrs. Burrell is over there now. Go get your snack and then join us upstairs on the poop deck."

Sidney cackled. He loved that word. "Okey dokey, Dad. See you in a jiff," Sid replied.

The crowd slowed us down as we tried to move up the narrow stairway. When we finally got to the outside deck, there were a hundred people squished together. Harry and I snaked our way through the crowd to where the anchor was hoisted.

"Wow!" I said, pointing out three things. "Look at the wake the ship makes! See Gillette's Castle on the hill

up there! Look! There's a swinging
bridge up ahead!"

Harry looked like he had just
stepped on glass in his bare feet. "Man,
this stinks! There's no room. I can't see
anything."

"Look at that cemetery, boys!" Mr. La Fleur said, pointing to the hill overlooking the river. "Lots of ancestors there!" He took a small camera out of his pocket and snapped some pictures. After a while, he checked his watch. "What's keeping Sid? We'd better go check on him at the snack shop."

After we followed him to the lower deck, I spotted Miss Mackle and Mrs. Burrell and our classmates. They were eating lunch and looking out the portholes.

"Isn't Sidney with you?" Mr. La Fleur asked as the ship dipped to the right.

"No. I thought he was with you," Mrs. Burrell answered. She was putting a wet towel over Dexter's forehead.

While Mr. La Fleur headed over to

the snack shop, Harry and I stayed and talked to Dexter. "What's wrong with you?" I asked.

"Aaaaaaugh," Dexter groaned.

"He's seasick," Mrs. Burrell explained.

"That's too bad," I said.

"Hey, Dex," Harry added, "if you can barf, you'll feel a lot better."

Suddenly, Mary and Ida screamed.

When we looked up, Song Lee was pointing at something floating in the water.

"Come and see!" they yelled.

Harry and I ran over to the portholes and looked.

There it was . . . bobbing in the water.

A sailor's hat.

The name *Sidney* was printed on it.

Sid the Squid,
Lost at Sea?

Miss Mackle came over immediately. When she saw the sailor hat floating in the water, she shuddered.

Harry didn't waste a second! First, he spotted the life jackets. They were stuffed inside the ceiling beams. Quickly, he hopped onto a chair, stood on his tiptoes, and reached the end strap of one life jacket. When it came tumbling

down, he caught it with both hands.
"I'll throw this to Captain Squid," he
said jumping to the floor.

Miss Mackle stopped him. "Harry
Spooger, what are you doing with that
life jacket? You already have one on!"

"I'm throwing it to Sid in the sea."

"Oh Harry!" Miss Mackle replied. "His father will find him. Sidney is probably just wandering around and his hat blew off. In the meantime, I'm asking the captain to page him. Now give me that life jacket, please. It's supposed to stay tucked in the ceiling for an emergency."

Harry reluctantly handed the teacher the life jacket. "Okay," he groaned.

Miss Mackle shook her head. "You know, Harry, you remind me a lot of your great-grandfather Sam Spooger. You really want to save someone."

Harry flashed his white teeth. "I *do!*"

Then Harry and I walked over to the boys' bathroom. We had to go. When we got there, we found a long line.

"Whoever is in there has kept us waiting now for five minutes," a father complained. He was holding a toddler who was pulling his hair.

Suddenly, Harry cut in front of everyone and banged on the door with his knuckles. *"Sid the Squid?"*

I smiled. Somehow that nickname seemed to fit Sid on the sea.

"Yeah?" a weak voice called back.

"That you?" I asked.

"No . . . it's . . . *me*."

When the door opened, we saw Dexter hobble out. His face looked sea green.

"I think . . . I feel . . . a little better," Dexter said. "I barfed."

As we took his arm and led him back to our class, we heard a voice come over the loudspeaker: *Will Sidney La Fleur please report to the snack shop immediately.*

Dexter ignored the announcement. "I guess . . . I can't rock at sea . . . like I can rock with Elvis," he mumbled.

"Speaking of music," I said. "Do you hear that?"

We stopped in our tracks and listened.

A pirate's tough but he can sing.
He wears a patch and a gold earring.
He climbs up rope and sails the sea
With a yo ho ho and a yo ho hee!

"Sidney!" we shouted. There he was, about five yards from the refreshment stand. A crowd of kids made a circle around him. You couldn't see Sid at all. You could just hear his sea chantey!

Mr. La Fleur, who was waiting by the
refreshment stand, looked over at us
immediately. When he saw us pointing
to the circle of kids, he ran right

through it. "Sidney! We've been looking all over for you. Didn't you hear the loudspeaker?" Then after he scolded him, he hugged him.

Sidney hugged him back. "I . . . didn't hear it. . . . I was singing."

"You shouldn't wander off like that!" Mr. La Fleur said as we all walked him back to our class.

When we returned, Dexter quietly sat down next to Mrs. Burrell. Everyone else yelled, *"Sidney!"*

Mary pointed to his ear. *"You stole Song Lee's earring!"*

"No! No I didn't!" Sidney replied. "I found it under the bus seat. I was just going to borrow it. I was planning all along to return it. I was just checking it out . . . like a library book."

Most of us rolled our eyes.

"So what do you say to Song Lee?" Mr. La Fleur asked.

"Sorry," Sidney said taking off the earring and handing it to Song Lee.

Mary shook her head. "If you really were a pirate like your ancestor Rupert, you would be marooned! Pirates aren't supposed to steal from each other."

Sidney wiped his eyes. "You're right. I should have asked first. Would you like a hot dog, Song Lee? I still have some allowance left."

Song Lee took a moment to think about it. "Yes, please," she said. "With mustard, relish, and ketchup."

"Okey dokey," Sid replied. Then he looked at the teacher. "Do you have an extra sailor's hat? I can't find mine."

Miss Mackle and Sid's stepdad exchanged a long look.

The last ten minutes of our trip, Mrs. Burrell asked, "Anyone want to see the view from the top deck?"

"Yeah!" Harry shouted.

Just as we were going up the winding stairwell, tons of people were coming down.

"It's raining!" they called.

Mary stopped in her tracks. "I'll stay downstairs. I don't want to get my new sailor's hat wet."

Sidney didn't have a choice. He was grounded next to his stepdad.

Dexter was asleep.

Mrs. Burrell looked at Song Lee, Ida, Harry, and me. "Do you mind a little rain?"

"Nah," Harry said. "Sailors like us are used to rain. Let's go!"

"My great-great-grandmother Persis sailed through icebergs and icy wind. Rain can't keep me from doing anything!" Ida exclaimed.

When we got to the top deck, we had the whole place to ourselves. What a view of the Connecticut River Valley!

"You know what, Harry?" I said. "I think we would have made it if we were on the *Titanic* or *Mayflower*. We're tough sailors."

"Yeah, we *are* tough sailors."

Ida handed her camera to her mother. "Please take a picture of Song Lee and me singing in the rain. I want to add it to Great-Great-Grandmother Persis's scrapbook."

"Good idea," Ida's mother replied.

While Mrs. Burrell snapped a picture of the girls, Harry and I looked over the railing. The raindrops hit the water like grains of sand.

"I love the sea," Harry said, taking a deep whiff of fishy air.

"Me too," I said, watching a bird flap its wings.

And then Harry yelled, *"Thanks Ida!"*

I don't think she heard Harry. Ida was too busy singing and dancing on the deck with her mother and Song Lee.